Thomas Docherty

Wash-a-Bye BEAR

templar publishing

"I love you, Bear," said Flora one morning.

"But Mummy says you are smelly and full of bits
and you need a wash."

"So you're going in the washing machine with all the dirty socks."

"Don't worry, Bear, I'm going to be right here waiting for you."

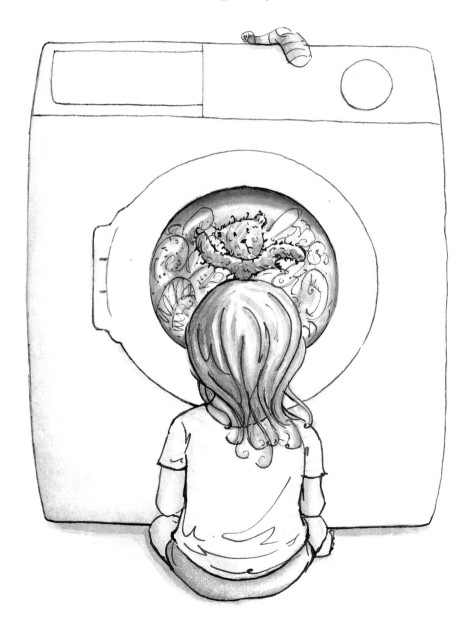

"Be brave, Bear!"

Wash away soggy breakfast smears...

wash away melted ice cream tears.

Wash away memories of the beach…

birthday cake and sticky sweets.

Wash away spatters of winter showers...

wash away mud and rain-soaked hours.

Wash away scrapes from climbing trees...

hide-and-seek in autumn leaves.

Wash away glittery glue from clothes...

wash away paint from paws and nose.

Wash away furious felt tip scribbles…

splats and spots and drips and dribbles.

And stop!

"Poor, brave, dizzy Bear."

"Clean, fluffy, wash-a-bye Bear."

"But now you don't look like Bear…

you don't smell like Bear…

you don't taste like Bear…

and you don't feel like Bear."

"Come on Bear,
I know what
to do."

Back through all our teatime fun,

every smear and every crumb.

Back through noisy garden games,

slippery slides and grassy stains.

Back through making things together, me and you for ever and ever.

And stop!

"Now you're my Bear again."

"But Mummy says now *I'm* all smelly and full of bits
so I need a wash, too."

"Mummy," said Flora after her bath. "Do you think Bear will still love me now that *I'm* all washed and clean?"

"Yes," said Mummy, "and he always will."